Me and My Social Media

Me and My Social Media

CLAIRE CAREY

CLOISTER HOUSE PRESS

First published in the United Kingdom in 2020 by
The Cloister House Press

ISBN 978-1-913460-08-2

Dedication

To family and good friends
xxx

'So, tell me, Bonnie. What's your group message all about?'

'Well, Auntie, it's just like having a group of friends in a room, all chatting.'

'Okay. Can anybody join the group?'

'No, Auntie. They have to be invited by another member of our group.'

'I see, Bonnie. So nobody can just walk into your room?'

'That's right, Auntie.'

'That's great – your group is a secret that only you know about.'

'That's right, Auntie.'

'Technology is a fantastic thing, Bonnie. I wish I could understand social media better.'

*

My Auntie Alice owns and runs the village shop in Peter's Green, the most beautiful place on the planet – that's what Auntie Alice told me anyway. The shop is very old-fashioned. Auntie will not sell carrier bags, so everybody who shops at Auntie's shop needs to bring their own bags. Auntie will not sell little bags of potatoes – you can only buy a paper sack. You cannot buy milk in plastic bottles, only glass, which is recycled and delivered fresh every day by the milkman. Auntie will not sell anything in plastic – fruit and veg is only sold in paper bags, and this how it has been since my grandparents owned the shop. Butter, cheese, ham all sold fresh, wrapped in greaseproof paper. By today's standards Auntie's shop is very fashionable.

Her husband Uncle Ron is a carpenter. He makes bespoke furniture, mainly special orders and one-offs. He works from home and has a gallery at the back of the house. It's all very exclusive.

Uncle Ron works very hard and really enjoys his work. Uncle Ron sends furniture all over the world, and to some very exclusive shops in London. Uncle Ron is a very kind man.

Uncle Ron and Auntie Alice don't have any children of their own, so they are always there for us – me fifteen, Violet fourteen, Francis eight, and Reggie five. I would say that Auntie Alice and Uncle Ron are very wealthy. Their house in Peter's Green is a very large house and stands in its own grounds very close to the shop. Auntie Alice has a full-time cleaner and gardener – however, if you didn't know that they were wealthy it would be hard to find out, because they are so modest. Auntie Alice's favourite shop is M&S, and Uncle Ron is always wearing overalls, and working. I have to say they are the best auntie and uncle you could ever wish for.

I help Auntie Alice in the shop on weekends. I don't get paid much because Auntie prefers to buy me presents – I suppose because she doesn't have any children of her own – but I don't mind.

My dad Charlie is a long-distance lorry driver. He owns his lorry and drives all over Europe and sometimes makes deliveries of furniture for Uncle Ron. In fact, Uncle Ron will only allow my dad to deliver his furniture. My dad can be gone for days at a time. My mum is a dressmaker by trade, and she works from home, like Uncle Ron except my mum has to do her work on the kitchen table. My mum works very hard. She also makes wedding dresses, which she designs herself. My mum's name is Grace, and Auntie calls my mum Amazing Grace, because she has four beautiful children. Auntie Alice is fifteen years older than my mum. Our house is small compared to Auntie's house, even though we have four bedrooms.

This weekend I'm helping Auntie at the shop. I'm not going out with my friends. The shop once belonged to Auntie's parents, my grandparents, so Auntie always helped out at the shop from a young age.

Auntie knows everybody in the village, and everybody

knows Auntie. My Mum said Auntie *is* the village. Without Auntie Alice, the village would not have any community left, apart from the village hall, and Auntie helps to keep that going with afternoon teas on Tuesdays and Thursdays, and dance club every Wednesday night.

Friday after school, our place was like a mad house: Violet was already home, Dad was away most of that weekend with the lorry, Auntie Alice had picked up the two youngest – Francis and Reggie – from school and brought them home, Mum had just made a nice cup of tea, Francis and Reggie were dancing and singing, then Violet was showing Auntie all her artwork. Mum still had all her stuff all over the dinner table because she was very behind with one of her dresses. Sometimes I wished I was a lorry driver so I could get some peace. I was going to stay at Auntie Alice's that night, ready for work in the shop the next day, and to get some peace. Auntie waited for me to pack my bag while she finished her cup of tea, and then we left.

I like staying at Auntie Alice's because I have my own bedroom, which Uncle Ron fitted out to perfection: beautiful wardrobes which Uncle Ron made himself, cream carpet and pink walls – and I even have my own bathroom. I feel like a princess. Auntie Alice really spoils us all. My mum lets Auntie do this because she doesn't have children of her own.

When we arrived at Auntie's house the electric gates opened and closed automatically. We drove down to the house, which was all lit up. My mum told me that Auntie Alice's house is off-grid. I asked my mum what that meant. Mum told me that Uncle Ron generates all his own electricity, so their house is self-sufficient, except for water. So without doubt it has to be the best house I've ever seen.

Uncle Ron was sat watching the TV. 'Hello, Bonnie.'

'Hello, Uncle Ron. Have you had a good week?'

'Not too bad, thank you.'

Auntie Alice went into the kitchen to make tea. I looked at my phone and saw eleven messages from my new group. They had given the group a name – G7, because there are seven girls in the group:

1. Saskia lives about three miles away, on Dean Farm. My mum and dad sometimes meet up with Saskia's parents and have evenings out. Saskia has even stayed over at Auntie Alice's with me at different times.
2. Beth lives at Chilton Green, also about three miles away. Nice girl, but very easily led.
3. Sacha lives in Luton, which is about ten minutes away. I met Sacha in school when she came to our school after being expelled from her first school. Sacha has only been at our school for eight months. My mum doesn't like me being friends with Sacha because we don't know her family.
4. Cath also lives in Luton. Her parents moved to Luton from Peter's Green because of work, so I have known Cath all my life. Cath lives next door to Sacha now, and I believe that's why Sacha came to our school – because Cath's mum helped get her in.
5. Vicky lives in Peter's Green, not too far from my house. I've never really gotten on with Vicky, but all the other girls like Vicky, so I don't say too much. My mum asked me not to be friends with her when we were in primary school, because she was a bully.
6. Larna lives in East Hyde, about two miles away. Larna is a very nice girl, quiet and kind.
7. That's me.

I start to respond to the message: yes, I liked the group name. It was agreed that nobody else could join our group, G7.

What's happening tomorrow? asked Beth. **We should meet up tomorrow.**

Six said yes … and then there was a no from me. Vicky was quick to ask me why not, so I replied that I was helping out in my Auntie's shop tomorrow.

Shame, said Beth.

Can you get out of it? asked Cath.

No, I replied.

Your auntie has loads of money. She can pay somebody else to do your job, said Vicky.

I didn't like this comment, to be honest, so I just replied, **Yeah, maybe.**

Nobody else said anything.

Saskia: **OK, ladies, where are we meeting?**
Larna: **You can all come over to my house. I've just asked my mum and she said it's OK for everybody to come to our house.**
Cath: **What can we do at your house? I would prefer to go into Luton town centre.**
Larna: **My mum will not allow me to go to Luton town centre.**
Sacha: 😄 😄 😄 **You are joking, right?**
Larna: 😄 😄 😄 **Yeah, only joking.**

I got the feeling she was not telling the truth, because Larna's mum is very strict and never lets her go too far away.

Saskia:	**Anybody fancy a day at the farm?**
Sacha:	😄 😄 😄
Cath:	😄 😄 😄
Sacha:	**Yeah, lets milk the cows … I don't think so. You lot are boring.**
Vicky:	**I'm not going to no farm on my day out.**
Larna:	**I'm not going to be able to come now because my grandparents are visiting, sorry girls.**
Saskia:	**That's lovely, Larna.**
Larna:	**Yes I'm looking forward to seeing them, my grandma has not been well, now she is feeling better she wants to see us all.**
Cath:	**Tell your mum you need to be with your friends tomorrow.**
Vicky:	**Yes make sure you tell your mum, you're going out, with us. Grandparents are boring.**
Larna:	**Look, I'm really sorry, but I cannot let my mum down.**
Cath:	**So you let your friends down instead Larna?**
Larna:	**I'm not coming out with you tomorrow and that's it.**

Good for you, Larna, I think to myself.

Sacha:	**Maybe we should change the name of the group to Sexy 6**
Vicky:	**Good idea** 😄 😄 😄
Cath:	**Some people just ain't got any respect.**

I had to say something.

Me:	**Oh, come on girls, that's not fair. Larna's grandma hasn't been well.**

Saskia:	**Yes, that's true.**
Me:	**I would want to see my grandma if she had been unwell.**
Sacha:	**OK, whatever.**
Cath:	**This time you choose your grandma, next time you choose your friends.**
Beth:	**So what is our plan, girls? Because it's getting late.**
Sacha:	**So what? Mummy putting you to bed?**
Beth:	**No, but if we don't get organised our day will be over.**
Vicky:	**You're right. I vote we all meet in McDonald's in town tomorrow at 12 noon**
Beth:	**Yes**
Vicky:	**Yes**
Cath:	**Yes**
Saskia:	**Yes**
Sacha:	**Yes**

I think to myself, I'm glad they've got that sorted. I hope the group gets a bit more friendly.

*

Auntie called me and Uncle Ron into the kitchen for tea. Auntie had made poached eggs on toast, my favourite, followed by banana split, Uncle Ron's favourite. We all sat down to enjoy our tea. Auntie Alice told Uncle Ron all about her day in the shop, and Uncle Ron told me all about his new pieces of furniture that he's making, and how some panels of wood needed to be changed because there were too many knots in the wood.

I love being at Auntie's. It's a home from home, and Auntie Alice and Uncle Ron are so kind, and although their house is a big house, it's very homely and welcoming, and I just feel so comfortable. Uncle Ron made most of the furniture, and what he couldn't make they bought from antique shops and second-hand and reclaimed materials. Uncle Ron is very cautious when it comes to the environment. Auntie Alice always tells us when it's mealtime that we can have what we want so long as we eat everything on the plate – Auntie Alice will not allow us to waste anything. Although they both spoil us, that's only through love and kindness.

After tea I cleaned up for Auntie and then we all went and watched TV in the living room. Auntie was reading her book while Uncle Ron was watching an old war film. Auntie has an open wood-burning fire, which Uncle Ron sees to every day. It looks lovely, and the crackles of the wood burning sound great. There are two three-seater sofas and one armchair for Uncle. After ten minutes watching TV, Uncle Ron fell fast asleep, so Auntie and I turned over the TV to watch *The Great British Bake Off* – both me and Auntie really like *Bake Off*. Just then, the phone rang. Auntie answered the phone: it was my mum.

Auntie was on the phone for about five minutes. When she'd finished, I asked Auntie, 'Is everything okay?'

'Yes, your mum was just making sure it was okay for Uncle Ron to look after Reggie and Francis tomorrow. Your mum was going to drop the two little ones off and now she needs Uncle Ron to pick them both up at 10am. Uncle Ron will probably take them down to Wardown Park for the day, so I will make them a packed lunch.' Auntie Alice told me about how Uncle Ron loved to visit Wardown Park. It reminded him of when he was a child, when his mum and dad would often take him there for the day.

Wardown Park is a beautiful park on the Bedford road in Luton. There are lots of things there, such as a boating lake which is full of ducks and swans, then there are playgrounds, a mini golf course, a museum, tennis courts, bandstand – it has everything you could ever want from a public park, set in the most beautiful grounds. It's a truly fantastic day out, and I know Francis and Reggie will have a lovely day with Uncle Ron.

My phone was on silent so as not to disturb anyone, but the messages were still coming through from my new group. It was mainly Sacha, Vicky and Cath. I couldn't really be bothered to read them – I was tired. Auntie Alice noticed that although my phone was on silent, every time a message came through it would vibrate.

Auntie said, 'You seem to be getting lots of notifications, Bonnie. Is everything okay?

'Yes, it's just my new group that we've started. To be honest, Auntie, earlier it all got a bit heated, so I'm not bothering anymore tonight.'

'I don't blame you. Tomorrow will be a better day.'

'I have some homework to do, so I will go to my room now, if you don't mind.'

'Good night, Bonnie.'

'Good night, Auntie.'

Uncle Ron was still fast asleep.

I put the TV on in my room and ran the bath. The bedroom is so nice. Auntie Alice and Uncle Ron really went out of their way to make me and my family welcome. I had a quick bath, cleaned my teeth, then did my homework for roughly an hour. I hope to be a teacher one day. I got into bed and my phone was still going, so I switched the phone off.

*

Next morning, at around 8.30, Auntie Alice woke me up with a cup of tea. I love a cup of tea in bed, and it's not something I get at home because my mum has so much to do first thing in the morning, so it's tea at the breakfast table with everybody else, which in all honesty is still very nice. I switched my phone back on and straight away it started to vibrate, as I still had the phone on silent.

9

They must have been up all night sending messages, I think. I didn't really want to look at the phone, but I did eventually and I was amazed: 122 messages! It was going to take me all day the read that lot. I was glad I switched off my phone. I got up and had a wash, made my bed and went down to the kitchen.

Auntie Alice and Uncle Ron were eating toast and drinking tea.

'What would you like for breakfast, Bonnie?' asked Auntie.

'Please could I have toast with strawberry jam?'

'Of course.'

Once breakfast was finished, Auntie made three packed lunches and puts them all in a cool bag and tells Uncle Ron he needs to pick up Francis and Reggie at 10 am from Grace's house. Then Auntie and I leave to go to the shop.

The shop isn't far from the house, so we could walk. On the way over, I started looking at my phone. The messages count was now up to 135. Thankfully they were only short, so I could sail through them. First it was all about what everybody was going to wear and they were all quite pleasant to each other, bearing in mind there were only five of them going out.

Next was discussing what each one of them was going to do with their hair, and what colour to paint their nails, and the colour of the lipstick, which shoes would go best with their outfits. They had all sent pictures of each other trying on their outfits. They'd been up all night – I noticed that the last message was sent by Sacha at 2.30 am. I was relieved to see that none of the messages were for me.

We arrived at the shop, which was already open. Auntie has a member of staff who opens the shop at 7 am every morning and takes all deliveries. The shop opens Monday to Saturday at 7.30 am and closes at 8 pm. Sunday opening is from 11 am to 2 pm. Once we arrived, Auntie took over the shop, and the member of staff left at 10 am (returning at 5 pm and staying until closing). Auntie leaves the shop at 5.30pm most days – this is a very good routine.

Just before I started work, I switched off my phone and packed it away safe. Each weekend my first job, sweep the floor, dust the shelves, clean windows. Once all the cleaning is done, I do a stock check, listing all items. After stock, I will make a few home deliveries, which is only around the village, walking-distance from the shop. I like doing the home deliveries because Peter's Green is a very nice place. Auntie told me we are the luckiest people in the world because we live in the most beautiful place, and I am grateful because in my heart I know Auntie is right. Auntie Alice and Uncle Ron have travelled all over the world, so they should know.

By the time all the deliveries were done, my shift was almost over. It was soon time for me and Auntie to return to her house. I was staying that night too, and my mum, Violet, Francis and Reggie were all staying over as well. Almost every Sunday we all have dinner together. My dad was still away, but he hoped to back in time for dinner.

We arrived back at the house and spotted Uncle Ron, Francis and Reggie all in the garden. Uncle Ron built the best treehouse you have ever seen, and Francis and Reggie are playing in it. Uncle was sat drinking a cup of tea, watching the kids.

'Have you had a nice day?' asked Auntie Alice.

'Yes,' replied Uncle Ron. 'The kids loved the park.'

'Did you go on the boats?'

'Yes, they made me row around the lake twice. The swan was chasing us, so the kids found it all very funny, but I felt like my arms were going to drop off, all that rowing.'

Just then, my mum and Violet arrived. My mum looked tired out.

It was a nice evening, so we all sat in the garden. Auntie suggested that we have takeaway for dinner.

'Fine with me,' said Uncle Ron.

'I'm happy with that,' said Mum.

I remembered my phone was still switched off, so I turned it back on: another 23 messages. OMG, I didn't know if I could keep this up. I looked through the messages and they were mainly photos of Beth, Saskia, Sacha, Cath and Vicky, all posing around town. Judging by the messages, they had all gone to the cinema.

*

'Takeaway's here! Everybody back in the house. Dinner as arrived!' called Auntie Alice. She had got the big table ready so we could all sit together. Uncle Ron dished up all the food, and my mum opened a bottle of wine.

I sat next to Violet. She and my mum had been doing the gardening today and tidying up all round the house. Mum looked so tired. I hoped Dad would be back in time for dinner the next day.

Violet liked drawing and painting and was really good at it. In fact, she spent most of her spare time drawing and painting. Uncle Ron put Violet's paintings in his gallery, and sometimes Uncle Ron sold them for Violet.

The takeaway went down well – all gone. Francis and Reggie went back into the garden to play in the treehouse. Violet and I cleaned up, and Mum, Auntie Alice and Uncle Ron went back into the garden to watch the kids. I get on well with Violet – she's a good sister. Although I'm the oldest, Violet seems older than me. She's very sensible and easy to get along with. Violet and her friends are goths – not into the heavy goth stuff, but still goth. Violet's friends are a nice group, very friendly, but goths tend to just stay within their own group because they all understand each other and they all like the same things.

Violet told me she was meeting up with her friends on the green later. Mum told Violet she could go to the green but she needs to be back at Auntie Alice's by 8.30 pm. One of Violet's friends Jan lives next door to Auntie Alice, so Violet would walk over to the green with him. In the winter Uncle Ron allows Violet and her friends to use his gallery to hang out. The gallery is very nice, with a TV and music system fitted. I overheard Uncle Ron tell my mum that he likes Violet's friends because they are all very polite, and when they leave the gallery you would never know they had ever been in there. 'Super bunch of kids,' said Uncle Ron. Violet was lucky to have such nice friends – which is more than I can say for me. Although Larna and Saskia are very nice, the rest are not so nice, which makes our group hard work.

*

Violet left to meet up with her friends, and Mum got Reggie and Francis in and took them upstairs to bath them. My mum has the biggest room at Auntie's house. Uncle Ron fitted the room with one double bed, and it has an adjoining room with bunk beds for Francis and Reggie, and a big bathroom. I think Uncle Ron and Auntie Alice would prefer us to live with them full-time; it's like the holidays for us, staying with them. My mum came back down after bathing the kids. 'Both Francis and Reggie went straight to sleep,' Mum said. 'They were so tired.'

We all settled in the living room and before long Uncle Ron was fast asleep just like Francis and Reggie, and Auntie was reading her book. Mum and Auntie finished the bottle of wine. I decided to take a look at my phone: another 31 messages. I hated to think it, but I couldn't be bothered with these messages – they all looked a bit aggressive. I wished I had never gotten into this. Looking quickly through, I noticed my name mentioned a couple of times.

Vicky: **What you up to, Bonnie???**

And then a few messages down, I saw Vicky continue: **Bonnie isn't answering us.**

Sacha:	**I bet her Auntie has locked her in the broom cupboard** 😄 😄 😄
Vicky:	**Best place for her** 😄 😄 😄
Saskia:	**Her auntie's lovely, she'd never do that.**
Sacha:	**And how do you know???**

I thought to myself that this group was bad, and wished I wasn't involved.

'Are you okay, Bonnie?' Mum said.

I pick my head up. 'Yes, Mum. Why?'

'Your face looks a bit worried.'

'No, I'm okay, Mum.'

'What were you looking at on your phone?'

'Oh, nothing, just Facebook and Snapchat.'

'Okay,' said Mum with a concerned look on her face.

The messages still kept coming through, my phone buzzing in my hand, which my mum had also noticed.

'It's nothing, Mum. Just Snapchat,' I lied.

I didn't want to tell my mum about the group because I knew that she wouldn't approve.

Just then, Violet arrived home right on time, just as she'd promised, 8.30pm. By then Uncle Ron had woken up.

'Hello, Violet. Have you been out with your friends?' he asked.

'Yes, Uncle Ron.'

'Are they all okay?'

'Yes, they're all fine.'

'That's good.'

Violet has her own room at Auntie's as well. It's exactly the same as mine.

Violet said, 'If you all don't mind, I'm going to my room. I have some drawings to finish.'

Everybody answered that it was fine.

*

I watched the TV some more and thought about how much I was looking forward to seeing my dad the next day. I hoped he got back in time for dinner. Auntie cooks the best Sunday dinner. She makes her own rice pudding and Yorkshires. Nothing frozen for Sunday dinner – Auntie makes sure it's all top-table for us.

'Well, I think I'm going to bed,' I yawned. 'Auntie, do you need me to go to the shop in the morning?'

'No, not tomorrow thanks, Bonnie, but could you and Violet do some cleaning here, upstairs?'

'Yes, of course. Do you need me to change the beds?

'Yes please,' replied Auntie.

'Okay. Good night, all,' I said, and I went up to my room.

On the way, I took one more look at my phone and noticed I only had 11 messages. I switched my phone off and got to bed.

*

The next day everybody got up and went down for breakfast. Auntie was already up, and she made the tea and toast for everybody – no tea in bed today because there were too many of us. After breakfast, Violet and I started cleaning upstairs. Auntie Alice is very organised upstairs: all cleaning materials are in a big double cupboard with all cleaning products necessary and a vacuum cleaner plus washing machine and tumble dryer, so within a few hours we had all the beds changed, the floors were cleaned, stairs done and bathrooms spotless, plus all the old bedding washed and packed away, easy. Both Violet and I know what we are doing, so the job gets done with ease, no chatting so we get the job done quicker.

15

By the time we were done, my dad was back. As we walked back downstairs he was sitting in the kitchen, drinking coffee with Uncle Ron, telling Uncle Ron all about his trip. He was really pleased to see me and Violet, and we were glad to have him home. My dad had brought us all a present each: I got a bag, Violet got a belt, Francis and Reggie got new lunchboxes. I could see my mum looked happier. My dad had been delivering furniture to Italy that week for Uncle Ron, so the two of them had a lot to talk about. Uncle Ron used to always deliver his own furniture, but these days that was not possible because all his time is taken up by the manufacturing side of things.

'Dinner's ready!' Auntie Alice tells everybody. 'All in the dining room, please.'

Francis and Reggie have to sit next to Dad. Auntie and my mum bring in the dinner. I love Auntie's Sunday dinner. The smell is delicious, and the taste is even better. I thought to myself that this was the best: Mum, Dad, Reggie, my sisters, Auntie, and Uncle Ron, all enjoying our Sunday dinner together. I felt very lucky to have such a loving and caring family. Auntie Alice and Uncle Ron are just like having another mum and dad, or I supposed the correct expression would be grandparents, but not really because our grandparents passed away many years ago. However, they are really good to us all, and I couldn't imagine my life without them.

Saskia and her mum were coming round after dinner, I looked forward to seeing Saskia. I would find out all about how her shopping trip went with the girls yesterday. Dinner was great, and then it was time for dessert. Auntie Alice always made her own rice pudding, which I have say is even better than dinner. Rice pudding is my dad's favourite, especially when Auntie Alice makes it herself.

*

After dinner Saskia and her mum Karen arrived. Karen is very nice – a kind, quiet woman, and very smart. My mum and Karen have been friends all their lives.

Saskia and I went up to my bedroom. Saskia seemed very quiet, so I asked her if she was okay. She started crying.

'OMG, what's the matter?'

Saskia started to tell me. 'Yesterday was terrible. Cath, Vicky, Beth and Sacha were getting up to all sorts of stuff. We've been banned from McDonald's because Sacha was throwing all the straws everywhere. She also emptied her drink all over the floor, and had a fight with the young lad cleaning the floor. I was so scared. The manager told us to get out or he was going to call the police. Sacha seemed to like this, and everybody who walked by was watching her, which made her worse. Honestly, I was terrified. If my mum and dad find out, they will be very upset. After McDonald's we went into Debenhams, and Vicky and Cath started to steal stuff. I asked them not to and then they got very aggressive with me. I felt very afraid so I ran away, and they ran after me, which made things worse. I couldn't get away.'

I said to Saskia, 'But I saw photos of you. You all looked okay.'

'Yes,' said Saskia, 'they *made* me do selfies and pretend I was happy, because they wanted to make you and Larna jealous.'

'Well, Saskia, that didn't work. I'm not jealous. I was very busy yesterday helping Auntie Alice with the shop, and family. In fact, I had a very nice day. I would definitely not swap my day for your day – it sounds terrible.

'It was,' Saskia said. 'I'm not going out with them again.'

'But did you go to the cinema, Saskia?'

'No. I was supposed to go, but unbeknown to the others, I called for a taxi, told them I was going to the toilet and ran for my life.

'OMG, this is shocking,' I said.

'Yes,' said Saskia. 'Look at the bruising on my arm from when we were in Debenhams and they dragged me back in there and tried to make me steal something.'

'OMG! How did you get out of that?'

'In the end I screamed out loud, "I'm not stealing anything!" and the security quickly ran over and told us all to get out – and this time I was pleased to be getting thrown out. I don't want anything else to do with them, but I feel afraid to leave the group.'

'Why?'

'Because they told me if I leave the group, that will be classed as disrespectful action to the group, and nobody disrespected us.'

Just then Saskia's mum called up, saying it was time to leave.

Saskia said, 'Please, please don't tell anyone. I'm afraid of what might happen to me.'

'Saskia, are you ready?' shouted her mum.

'No, don't worry, your secret is safe with me,' I said. Then I gave her a hug. Saskia was shaking. 'I promise I won't tell anyone.'

*

When Saskia had left, I sat there, feeling very sad for her. It must have been terrible, I thought to myself. I could not help but feel that I wished I'd never gotten involved with the group, and I wondered how I was going to get out of it.

Saskia seemed very afraid, and I hoped she would be okay in school the next day.

I went back downstairs to find everybody sat in the garden. Violet was painting, Francis and Reggie were playing on the swings, and Mum and Auntie were sat chatting. Dad and Uncle Ron were talking about next week's deliveries, which were all going to be in the UK.

'Okay, girls – and you, Reggie – it's time to go home,' said Mum a few moments later. 'Please can you collect your stuff and make sure you don't leave anything behind.'

We all packed up and set off. Uncle Ron and Auntie Alice looked tired when we left. We all had an early start the next day, except Dad: he would be washing and polishing his lorry all day. Dad loves his lorry. My dad doesn't work Mondays, but he starts at 4am Tuesdays.

Once we arrived home, Mum made us all tea while Violet and I made sure all our uniforms were ready for the morning, and I also made sure Francis and Reggie's school bags were all in order. Dad was listening to Francis read – Francis is a free reader now so my dad enjoys listening to Francis read.

*

The next morning, it was chaos: everybody up, breakfast, toast, jam, cereals, porridge, bagels – you name it, Mum has got it. Dad took me and Violet to school, we never needed to get the bus on Mondays, and Mum took the little ones in. I wasn't looking forward to seeing the group, and on the way to school Dad asked me if I was okay.

'Yes, Dad. I'm fine.'

'Okay,' said Dad. 'You just seem quiet, Bonnie.'

'I'm okay, Dad.'

We arrived at school. Violet went off to her class and I went to mine. On the way to class the first person I ran into was Vicky – she was late for her class so there was no time to chat, and I was glad, because I don't see eye-to-eye with Vicky most of the time.

School was pretty straightforward that morning, and lunchtime soon came around. As soon as I walked into the dinner room, I noticed Saskia was sitting on her own, so once I got my lunch I went and sat next to her. As I walked over, I could see the look of relief on her face.

'Are you okay?' I asked.

'Not bad, thanks,' she replied.

Saskia asked me, 'Have you seen any of the group?'

With that, Larna walked over. She noticed that Saskia looked worried. 'Are you okay, Saskia?' she asked.

Saskia nodded her head and quietly said, 'Yes.'

'Are you sure? You look worried.'

I could see Saskia's eyes filling up. Larna sat down on the other side of Saskia. Saskia told Larna, 'It's the group. I want to leave, but I feel I will be letting you down.'

Larna said, 'Me too. It's all a bit aggressive for me.'

I asked Larna, 'How's your grandma?'

'She's very well, thank you for asking. I was glad my grandma visited, because I didn't want to go out with the group after those messages.'

Saskia said, 'I wished that I had never gone out with them Saturday.'

'Why?' Larna asked.

Saskia replied, 'It's a long story.'

Just then, I noticed Vicky, Sacha and Beth talking to my sister Violet and her friends, and then they turned and walked over to us.

'Hey Bonnie, you never said your sister was a goth,' said Sacha.

I replied, 'I didn't know you knew my sister, Sacha.'

'I didn't, but I do now. Vicky told me all about and her and her friends.'

I looked at Vicky and she was laughing, I didn't like this conversation, I thought to myself.

Sacha then asked, 'Have any of you seen Cath?'

I quickly replied that I hadn't, followed by Larna and Saskia.

Vicky then sat down next to Larna. 'So, Saskia, what

happened to you Saturday?' she asked. 'We looked for you everywhere.'

Saskia quickly replied, 'My mum sent a taxi for me because I felt sick.'

I thought to myself, what a clever answer – well done, Saskia.

Saskia then had a look of relief on her face. She had managed to get herself out of any rubbish Vicky was about to throw at her.

Just then, Cath arrived. 'I'm calling a group meeting after school. We need to make sure everybody is on board with G7,' she said.

'Yes,' said Vicky, 'straight after school.'

Sacha told us we are meeting at, 'Front gate, 3.15 pm, no excuses. We need to get this pretty group into shape.'

I had the feeling they had already had a meeting without us being present. With that in mind, it was time to return to class.

On my way back to class I could not help thinking something bad was going on within the group and that Sacha and Vicky had something planned for me, Saskia and Larna. It was also clear to me that the group was in two halves: me, Saskia and Larna on one side, and Sacha, Vicky, Cath and Beth on the other side. It was also clear to me that Saskia, Larna and I really wanted to get out of the group. In fact, we had really been tricked into the group.

*

In my class I found it hard to concentrate, and the afternoon seem to drag.

The school day finally finished and it was time to meet the group. I was filled with dread as I left my class, thinking more about Vicky, Sacha, Cath and Beth. I was never best friends with those four. It all started about six weeks ago, when all four of them would get on our bus home. Sacha and Cath would stay over at Vicky's house, and sometimes they would invite me, Larna and Saskia. We never turned down the invites because we were getting on okay with them all. However, they never did get the same bus before – they would always get the later bus. Once they started getting the same bus as me, Saskia and Larna, they somehow befriended us, lulling us into a false sense of security. Now I realised what they had done, I had to find a way to get me, Saskia and Larna out.

I arrived at the meeting place, and Vicky was already there, and I could see Beth in the distance.

I asked Vicky, 'What's this meeting about?'

She replied, 'You will have to see.'

With an answer like that, it was clear she already knew.

I told Vicky, 'Well, I hope it's not going to take too long, because I need to catch my bus.'

Vicky replied, 'If you hadn't disrespected G7 in the first place, everything would be fine.'

I didn't answer this, because Vicky was trying to provoke an argument within.

By then, Beth was standing by my side, looking as gullible as always. Beth is a nice girl, but you could tell her that Martians lived on the moon and she would believe you. Next Larna arrived, Saskia was in sight, and Sacha had also arrived. We were just waiting for Cath to arrive.

Saskia asked how long we were going to be, because the bus would arrive in twenty minutes. I agreed with Saskia, because I went home on the same bus.

Sacha replied, 'Look, girls, it's like this now. G7 is all you need to care about – not your fucking bus, not your mum or dad. G7 is all you need to know.'

I was shocked by Sacha's attitude. I looked at Saskia. She was shaking.

As Cath arrived, she looked at Saskia and said, 'It looks like the meeting has already started.'

Sacha started laughing.

Cath shouted in Larna's face, 'You will do just what I say from now onwards!'

Larna went bright red with temper, and I thought she was going to slap Cath, but she just took a step back.

Vicky confirmed that Sacha and Cath were the leaders of G7 and that we had to obey everything they said, no excuses. Sacha and Cath would have full control of G7 from then on. I looked at Sacha and Cath and told them I was leaving G7. Cath and Sacha came up close to my face and Sacha shouted, 'That's what you think! You joined this group and you are not leaving.'

Larna and Saskia had gone white with fear. I looked at Larna and Saskia and just shook my head. I then told them, 'I have my mum, dad and a very good family. I don't need you, and I don't care about this group. I'm leaving, and that's it.'

Vicky, who knows all my family and history, said, 'Bonnie, if you leave this group, bad things can happen to your family.'

I looked at Vicky and said, 'Yeah? And what are you going to do? Because I also know your family, in case you forgot.'

Vicky quickly shut up and put her head down. I felt very pleased with myself.

Larna said, with a worried look on her face, 'Come on, girls, let's all be friends. There's no need for this kind of behaviour.'

Sacha said, 'Yes, let's all be nice and friendly – if you do what you're told.'

It was clear to me that Sacha, Cath, Beth and Vicky had a hidden agenda for me, Saskia and Larna.

I said, 'I'm leaving, and that's it. My bus will be here in five minutes. Are you coming, Saskia?'

Saskia quickly replied, in a relieved tone of voice, 'Yes, I'm coming with you.'

We turned and walked away, followed by Larna. Sacha shouted to us, 'If you think you're just walking out, you can think again. I'll see you tomorrow.'

*

On our way home, we decided not to tell our parents about the group – which would turn out to be a very big mistake. Larna said we should create our own chat group so that we could stay connected all the time. I could see that Saskia and Larna were really worried in case there was any physical violence. Sacha is quite a big girl who comes across as being very strong; Vicky was already famous in our area for being a tough bully; and Cath had become altogether different since she left Peter's Green. She'd always been straightforward, and I always got on quite well with her before she moved away from Peter's Green, but since she left, Cath had adopted another personality which was quite wild, to say the least. And Beth is any-which-way-the-wind-blows; she will just do as she is told and you cannot help her to see sense.

I told Saskia and Larna not to worry too much, but I could see that they were in fact very scared and worried about going to school the next day.

Once we got to Peter's Green, we all went our separate ways. Violet, Francis and Reggie were already home. As soon as I walked through the door, my mum asked me if I was okay.

'Yes, I'm fine.'

'Is everything okay with school?'

'Yes,' I replied.

'Dad said you were a bit anxious this morning when he dropped you off at school?'

I changed the subject quickly. 'Will Auntie Alice need me this weekend in the shop?'

'No, not this weekend,' said Mum, 'so you're free to spend time with your friends.' Mum must have seen the look on my face when she mentioned friends. 'I take it everything is okay with your friends, Bonnie?' Mum asked.

I replied, 'Yes.'

Violet quickly picked her head up and said, 'Your friend Sacha spoke to me at lunchtime, and I don't like her. She made fun of my friends.'

I quickly replied, 'Take no notice. She's like that. She didn't mean any offence.'

'Well, it never sounded like that, Bonnie. I don't like her.'

'No,' said Mum. 'That girl is trouble, if you ask me.'

I reassured Mum that everything was okay and went off to do my homework.

My dad had decided to leave earlier with the lorry. This time he was driving up to Scotland and back, so all being well he would be back the next day.

I got up to my room, which I shared with Violet. I got stuck into my homework to take my mind off what had happened that day. I thought to myself, *I know what happened today was not good, but hopefully it will blow over – and I'm out of the group anyway.* Just then, I remembered I needed to remove myself from the group on my phone, so I picked up my phone and brought up the group. There were forty-four unread messages. I changed my mind; I realised that if I left the group, I wouldn't know what was going on, so for the benefit of Saskia and Larna I would stay in, even though I didn't want to.

I started to look at the 44 unread messages. What a joke – they really don't have anything to do or think about except making trouble. I thought to myself, how on earth did I get involved with this? Well, I didn't; they got me involved. Saskia and Larna only send messages to make sure we all got the bus to school at the same time.

Violet came upstairs. It was time for bed.

'Be careful with those friends,' Violet said.

I replied, 'I know they're spiteful, and I'm trying to get away.'

'What do you mean "trying to get away"?' asked Violet.

I told Violet about the group being aggressive, and that I wanted to leave.

Violet replied, 'Just leave, then.'

I replied, 'I wish it was that easy.'

Violet shook her head.

'It's a long story,' I said.

'You need new friends, Bonnie. Saskia and Larna are good friends and I really get on okay with them too, but the rest are just up to no good and they are trying to drag you, Saskia and Larna down.' Violet repeated herself: 'Just be careful.'

'I will. Good night.'

'Good night, Bonnie.'

*

Next morning, as I went downstairs for breakfast, Auntie Alice was sitting at the kitchen table, drinking a cup of tea.

'Morning, Auntie.'

'Morning, Bonnie. I'm taking you to school today.'

'But I've made arrangements to get the bus with Saskia and Larna.'

'That's okay,' said Auntie. 'We will pick them up from the bus stop.'

I smiled and said, 'Thank you.'

After breakfast we left, me and Violet got into the car and Auntie driving us straight to the bus stop. Saskia was waiting and Larna was just approaching, and they both got into the car and we left. I could see that Saskia and Larna were very pleased that Auntie was taking us to school.

On the way to school we drove past the bus stop where we'd

get off for school, and Sacha, Vicky, Cath and Beth were stood waiting there.

Auntie noticed them straight away. 'Is that Vicky and Cath?' she asked.

'Yes,' I replied.

Auntie asked me, 'Why would they be waiting at the bus stop?'

'No idea,' I replied.

Saskia and Larna had that worried look on their faces again, and Auntie noticed that too. Auntie started to drive her car around to the car park, so I told her she could just drop us off by the front.

Auntie replied, 'No, I have the time today, so I'm going to take a look around.'

Larna and Saskia had a look of relief on their faces.

We all walked around to the main entrance. There was no sign of Sacha, Vicky, Cath and Beth. I thought to myself that they wouldn't have recognised Auntie's car, so they wouldn't have seen us driving by, so hopefully they would wait at the bus stop all day.

Auntie didn't mention anything about my friends or my group, so I'm guessing my dad told mum about me looking anxious yesterday, then, I would imagine, Violet told Mum about her encounter with Sacha, and I was slightly late yesterday getting home. My mum would have phoned Auntie with her concerns.

Auntie watched us all go through the doors, and then she left.

*

School was pretty straightforward again that morning, and it was soon time for lunch. Before going into the dinner room, I met Saskia and Larna so we could all walk in together. Larna asked me if my auntie knew our situation, and I replied that I

27

hadn't said anything but that my dad had picked up on my anxiety on the way to school yesterday.

Saskia said, 'I'm glad your Auntie brought us to school today.'

Larna said, 'Do you think they were waiting at the bus stop for us?'

I replied, 'Yes, because the bus had gone and Vicky was there.'

'Saskia said Vicky stayed over at Cath's last night,' said Larna. 'Vicky has been doing that quite a lot these days. She told me it's easier for school, and her mum doesn't mind her staying away.'

We walked into the dinner room and straight away we could see Sacha, Vicky, Cath and Beth all sat together. They looked straight at us as if they had been waiting for us. We got our lunch and sat down, trying our best to keep as far away as possible. As soon as we all sat down, Sacha and Vicky came straight over to us.

Vicky asked us, 'How did you get to school today?'

I quickly replied before anybody else could say anything: 'We got the early bus.'

Saskia chimed in, 'Yes, I needed to do catch-up.'

'And me,' said Larna.

Vicky replied, 'Shame. We were waiting for you to arrive.'

Then Sacha said, 'We need to talk to you three.'

I turned to Sacha and said, 'We did all our talking yesterday.'

Larna said, 'I've got to go straight home tonight. My mum is going out.'

Saskia then said, 'We don't want to be in the group anymore.'

Sacha looked at Saskia and said, 'What, you speak for everybody now, Saskia?'

'No, but we have just had enough of being in the group. It's not for us.'

Sacha looked so angry. 'Well, I have plans for you three, so you're staying in the group, and if you leave, bad things will happen to your families.' By the look on her face she wasn't joking.

This was the first time I'd really felt fear. Saskia was also shaking, and Larna just started crying. The teacher on duty noticed that something was wrong, so she came straight over and asked what was going on. The teacher told Sacha and Vicky to return to their seats. They gave the teacher a dirty look and walked back over to where they had been sitting. The teacher turned to us and asked what was going on.

Larna was still crying and Saskia was as white as a ghost, and I must have looked like I was in shock. The teacher called for the headteacher to come straight to the dinner room. Within five minutes the headteacher was in the dinner room talking to the teacher, and after they finished chatting, the headteacher went straight over to Sacha, Vicky, Cath and Beth – but the four girls got up and walked out of the dinner room before she had reached them.

I heard the head teacher saying, 'And just where do you think you're going?' but the girls never looked at the headteacher and never replied; they just walked out.

The headteacher then came over to us and asked us to come to her office after we had finished our lunch. We didn't eat our lunch; we just went straight to the office. On the way to the office I realised that I hadn't seen Violet in the dinner room. Maybe she went to the chip shop. Sometimes Violet goes there instead of school dinners.

We got to the headteacher's office.

'Come in, girls. Sit down.' Mrs May is a nice lady, and when I walked into the office I could see that she was concerned. 'Okay, girls, do you have an explanation for me?'

Saskia spoke first. 'Well, Miss, it all started when we got involved with a group chat called G7.'

'Okay, Saskia, and who is in this group?'

'Us three, and Sacha, Beth, Vicky and Cath. At first, Miss, everything seemed fine, but then last Saturday I went into town with Sacha, Vicky, Cath and Beth, and they started to make trouble in town. I tried to get away, but they pulled me back. In the end I managed to get away by calling for a taxi.'

Mrs May looked shocked. She turned to me and asked me, 'What is your involvement, Bonnie?'

'Well, Miss, I'm just in the group. I couldn't go with them on Saturday.'

Mrs May asked, 'When did you start this group?'

'Only last week.'

'And were you all friends before?'

'Yes, and everything was okay before we started the group, but since the group started, Sacha, Vicky, Cath and Beth are trying to control us.'

'And Larna, what have you to say about this group?'

'Well, Miss, all what Saskia and Bonnie have said, I'm in the same position. But I feel very afraid. I wasn't able to go on Saturday because my grandparents were visiting, and the girls made me feel like I was being disrespectful to the group. I explained that my grandma had been unwell and I really wanted to see her, but they weren't bothered and made me feel terrible for wanting to see my grandparents.'

'I've got the picture,' said Mrs May, 'and I'm very concerned about you three. Have you told your parents?'

'No,' said Larna. 'We are all too afraid.'

Mrs May went on. 'Well, girls, I'm afraid if what you have told me is true, this is a really serious matter. I'm not doubting you, but as the headteacher I will need to speak to Sacha,

Vicky, Cath and Beth, because I cannot be seen to take sides right now. I have to remain neutral at this point. You must tell your parents straight away. We can only protect you whilst you are within the school grounds. As the headteacher, I've been through these types of problems before, and these situations can get very out of control if you don't stop them.'

Mrs May turned to me. 'Bonnie, I noticed your Auntie Alice here this morning. Is this the reason why?'

'I think so, Miss. My dad brought me and Violet to school yesterday, and he noticed I was anxious, so he must have told my mum, and my mum must have told Auntie Alice. Auntie Alice brought us three and Violet to school this morning.'

Mrs May asked, 'Who's picking you up?'

Saskia replied, 'We were supposed to get the bus home today.'

Mrs May told us, 'I'm going to contact all your parents and make the arrangements for you to be collected from my office. Did you know, Bonnie, that me and your Auntie Alice went to school together?'

'No I didn't know that, Miss.'

'One more question,' said Mrs May. 'Has Violet had any involvement in this group?'

'No,' I replied.

'That's good,' said Mrs May. 'Okay, girls, you can return to class. Once you have finished class, please come back to my office, and you will be picked up from here, and I'm going to get a message to Violet to meet you all here.'

We all thanked Mrs May and left the office. We all felt much better.

*

In class I couldn't help thinking about Violet. I wished that I'd seen her in the dinner room, but hopefully Violet had been in there and I just never noticed her with all the commotion.

31

Mrs May was most helpful. I was also really glad that she knew Auntie Alice personally, so that when Mrs May phoned my mum she would be able to put her mind at rest and let her know that we were all fine. I wasn't looking forward to telling my mum and dad about what had been going on. I knew that my mum didn't like me being friends with Sacha. Sacha had already been expelled from her first school, and my mum said that she didn't know Sacha's parents, and my mum always made sure that she got to meet our friends' parents and exchange contact details, and this way they would also then get to know my mum as well. My mum insisted that this was the right way to do things.

The afternoon seemed to drag, and the only thing I could really think about was Violet.

*

Before my classes ended, my mum and auntie were already in school. I saw my mum's car pull up outside, and I filled with dread. I felt like I had let my mum and dad down badly. My lessons finally ended and I made my way back to Mrs May's office.

As I approached the office, the first thing I noticed was the police going into Mrs May's office, and I could see my mum and auntie outside of the office, and another member of staff was sitting with my mum. Auntie was on the phone and pacing the floor at the same time. I sensed we had a problem.

Just then, Larna and Saskia approached me, and we all arrived outside of the office at the same time. My mum was crying, and I sensed Auntie was very angry.

'Bonnie,' Auntie said with a stern tone of voice, 'did you see Violet in the dinner room today?'

My whole body felt like it was draining and then I felt sick. I replied, 'NO, I didn't see Violet, Auntie.'

I knew what was coming next. I looked at Larna and Saskia and just started crying like my mum was crying.

The police were in Mrs May's office, going through the CCTV, Auntie told me. I overheard the member of staff telling my mum that they were trying to get a clear image of Violet. The whole thing was taking all my breath, and I felt like I was suffocating.

Saskia and Larna told me to sit down, but I didn't want to sit down. I just wanted my sister Violet to walk round the corner. Please, Violet. PLEASE. But there was no sign of Violet.

Saskia asked if she could go into Mrs May's office.

We all looked at Saskia as if to say, 'but the police are in there', and without us saying anything, Saskia said, 'I know the police are in the office, but I want to tell them something we never told Mrs May earlier.'

The member of staff who was sitting with my mum said, 'Come with me,' and they went straight into Mrs May's office.

I started thinking fast to myself what Saskia could want to tell the police that we never mentioned to Mrs May, and then it came to me: we never mentioned to Mrs May that Sacha told us that if we didn't co-operate with her, then bad things would happen to our families. I remembered the look on Sacha's face – a look of pure evil, as if she had been possessed by the devil himself. I hoped that was what Saskia was telling the police. They needed to know everything. I looked around and it felt like the room was spinning, like I was in a bad dream and I couldn't wake up, even though I was trying so hard.

Then I thought: My dad. I need my dad. When will he be home? Tonight? My mum must have read my mind. 'Bonnie, please don't mention any of this to your dad yet. He should be home later today.'

I replied, 'Don't worry, Mum. I won't.'

Auntie had been on the phone, making sure Uncle Ron

would pick up Francis and Reggie from school and take them to our home in case Violet showed up at home.

Just then, the police came out of Mrs May's office and spoke to Auntie Alice. Saskia's mum arrived, looked around and sat with my mum. Larna's mum was still on her way.

Saskia came over to me and told me that she had told the police about what Sacha said in the dinner room, that bad things could happen to our families if we didn't do what she said. I replied, 'Thank you.'

Mrs May asked Saskia's mum to come into her office. She looked at my mum and said, 'I will be back in a minute.'

*

The police told my Auntie Alice that the two incidents – one being the trouble in the dinner room and the other being Violet not coming back after lunch – may not be linked. The officers also told Auntie, 'Having said that, we don't leave anything to chance.' The police officer also said, 'It's still very early in the day, so our advice is to go home, because Violet may well be home. This is your case number, and a direct phone number, so if Violet is at home, you must call us straight away. We have managed to get a good picture of Violet from the CCTV, but please could you email across the most recent photos you have of Violet, one in school uniform and one in casual clothing.' The officer continued, 'We don't normally attend incidents in school unless it's violent. However, Mrs May insisted that we attend as soon as possible because of the nasty group that you three girls have gotten involved with. We are also aware that Violet is very punctual, so this is out of character for her, not to be back in school after lunch. With everything considered, that's all we can do at this time. But one more thing – Saskia, Bonnie and Larna, please switch off your phones, until we can collect them. Also, if you're going anywhere, please make sure your parents know where you are at all times. Personally I would like to tell you to stay at home until Violet is found, but I'm not allowed to do that. We will keep you informed of any updates.'

With that, the police left. I felt like I wanted them to stay. I watched them leave until I could no longer see them, and once they were gone, I felt like my safety net was gone from underneath me, and I was walking the tightrope and was about to fall off. I felt like crying out to the police officer, 'Please come back!' – but they was gone, and I couldn't see them anymore.

Larna's mum arrived. She was so angry and expressed it very verbally. 'I told you, Larna, to stay away from them girls. You never got on with Vicky. She was a very spiteful little girl, and Vicky hasn't gotten any better with age.' Larna's mum then turned to my mum and said, 'I'm very sorry, but I'm just so angry. What have the police said?'

Auntie told Larna's mum, 'They have said the best thing to do is go home. Ron is already home, and Violet's not there. Ron has driven all round the village, and there is no trace of Violet anywhere.'

Just then, Violet's schoolfriends walked over to us, in our cluster around the headteacher's waiting area. As they were walking towards us, I started to cry. The friends were all very upset too.

One of them said, 'We all know Violet, and this isn't like her to just go off.'

He unfolded a slip of paper. Violet's friends had all written their names and addresses down, and the boy handed it to Auntie in case the police wanted to talk to them at any time. They told Auntie and my mum that they had all tried to contact Violet, but she hadn't responded to any of them.

One of them said, 'If you need us to help in any way, please don't hesitate to ask us. Violet is the nicest person we know.'

35

Mum couldn't thank them enough. 'You beautiful children. Thank so much.'

Auntie asked them to pray for Violet with positive energy, and they all agreed, and they left.

It was so painful to look at Violet's friends and see that Violet was not with them.

*

It was time to leave the school – there was no point in remaining. Mrs May came out and saw us off.

'I don't expect the three girls to be in school tomorrow, if that helps,' she said to our mums. 'And Alice, please keep me informed.'

Auntie nodded. 'I will, Rose, and thank you for your support today.'

Saskia's mum and Larna's mum were also coming back to our house. Auntie drove us in Mum's car, while Mum looked at everything as we drove past. 'Keep looking, Bonnie,' she said. 'You might just see Violet somewhere.'

I was looking so hard for Violet. *Please, please, please, Violet, be round the next corner.*

Auntie was driving as slow as possible. We really didn't want to go home. My mum must have phoned Uncle Ron ten times, just to check Violet hadn't turned up. My dad had been in contact with Mum just to let her know he would be home around 5.30. How would Mum break this to Dad? The pain was unbearable. After the longest drive ever, we arrived home.

I walked into the house and Uncle Ron was as white as a sheet. I had never seen Uncle Ron look ill before, and I felt like crying again, but this time I managed to hold it in for Uncle Ron's sake. Violet was his favourite. As soon as we all got through the door of the house, Uncle Ron couldn't sit still. 'I've got to go and look for her. I'm not sitting here doing nothing.'

Auntie asked him, 'Have you got your phone?'

'Yes' – and Uncle Ron was gone.

Everybody sat down, and I made a cup of tea for everybody. Auntie was straight back on the phone, letting everybody know and asking them to keep an eye out for Violet. My mum was very irritable and restless. Saskia's mum was organising a search team for first thing the next morning, 6 am to 8 am, two hours of searching before anybody started work. Larna's mum was putting labels on our phone, ready in case the police needed them tomorrow. Larna's mum also suggested that we removed anything a bit personal and that was not relevant.

*

Uncle Ron knew a private investigator and had already been on the phone to him, and Auntie had to go home because the investigator was coming round to get all the details. Auntie asked me to go with her because although the police had told us that the group message may not be anything to do with Violet going missing, Auntie's investigator didn't want to leave any stone unturned.

Auntie had managed to get all the details from the CCTV in school, and she had photos of Violet ready. We arrived at Auntie's house, and as we drove in through the gate, right behind us was the investigator.

Auntie Alice went through everything with Mr Kray, and he then turned to me. 'Please, Bonnie, can I see your phone?'

I handed over my phone and the investigator started reading the messages. After about five minutes, he handed the phone back and told me not to lose the messages, and to back them up, if I could.

'What do you think?' asked Auntie.

'Well, those messages show plenty of aggression and arrogance, but they don't prove anything.'

'Bonnie, please tell Mr Kray about the meeting your group

had, and tell Mr Kray all about what happened in the dinner room,' Auntie said.

I went over everything again, from start to finish.

After an hour of me covering every detail, Mr Kray thanked me and told Auntie, 'I have everything I need for now. If Violet doesn't show up tonight and the police have to visit tomorrow, please let me know the outcome, and hopefully if Violet comes home, please let me know straight away.'

And with that, Mr Kray left.

Auntie packed an overnight bag and we went back to my house. I asked Auntie if the shop was okay, and Auntie replied, 'Yes, I've organised the shop so I don't have to go there.'

*

As we returned to my house, I could see that my dad's lorry was back. I felt a kind of relief and dread at the same time – such a sick feeling which is hard to explain. As we walked into the house, Reggie and Francis were sitting with Dad. I had forgotten all about Reggie and Francis – how could I do that? They must be so confused.

My dad looked like he was in complete shock. He got up and walked over to me, put his arms around me, and I felt my legs give way as if somebody had pulled them away from me, and I fell to the floor.

'I'm so sorry, Dad. This is all my fault.'

'No, Bonnie, it's not your fault. I'm sure Violet will be back soon.'

By then, Saskia and her mum and Larna and her mum had left.

My dad turned to Auntie Alice. 'Where's Ron gone to look for Violet?'

'I'm not sure, Charlie,' Auntie replied.

My mum and dad wanted to know what the investigator had said. Whilst they were all talking about that, I went and sat with Reggie and Francis and watched the TV. Reggie asked me if we could go and look for Violet. Holding back tears, I told him that we needed to stay indoors so we could make her a cup of tea when she got home. Reggie agreed.

Francis said, 'Can we go and tidy up your room so that it's ready for when Violet comes home?'

I had to think fast. 'I think it's best to leave our room just the way it is, because Violet won't be pleased with us if we move her stuff around.'

'Okay,' said Francis. 'I love Violet. She always helps me with my homework, not like you.'

'I know, Francis, but I do have my own stuff to do.'

*

Uncle Ron got back. He walked in, looking shocking, and was followed by some of Violet's friends from the green. They had been with Uncle Ron, into Luton town centre looking for Violet, and had stopped at all the little villages on the way back to Peter's Green. By that time, the sun was starting to set. My mum made all Violet's friends a cup of tea and sandwiches. Everybody was checking their phones, looking for clues. All of Violet's friends looked completely gutted.

'We couldn't find anything online or in messages to suggest that Violet was going to wander off,' one of them said. 'Everything looked normal.'

The darker it got, the harder it became to search the streets, but my dad and uncle went back out to look again. Before Violet's friends left our house, they told my mum that they would not stop looking for Violet until she was found, and they all took my mum's phone number so that if Violet made any contact with any of them, they could let my mum know straight away. My mum thanked them all, and Auntie asked them all to pray for Violet because we needed positive thoughts, and once again they all agreed with Auntie and they all left.

I decided to take Reggie and Francis upstairs to get them ready for bed. Once Reggie and Francis were washed, they both made themselves comfortable in Francis's bedroom and put on the TV. Reggie told me he was going to sleep with his fingers crossed so that when he woke up, Violet would be home. Francis told me that she would be saying prayers so that Violet would be home first thing in the morning.

I went back downstairs. My mum and auntie were pacing the floor. You could taste the anxiety in our house.

Just before dark, the police called to inform us that they would be at our house by 8 am the next morning. They also told my mum that every patrol car in the county that was out on duty that night had a photo of Violet. My mum had a slight look of relief on her face when she explained this to Auntie. Auntie replied, 'Well, that's something positive.'

My mum asked me if I thought this had anything to do with Sacha, Vicky, Cath and Beth.

I replied, 'Yes, I think they have something to do with this situation.'

Auntie asked, 'Do you think they're capable of hurting her?'

'I don't think they'll hurt Violet. They will use Violet to get to us. Once the police collect the phones tomorrow, they will be able to start to contact Vicky, Sacha, Cath and Beth for questioning. But let's hope Violet is home before then.'

My dad returned home at that point. He looked like a lost man. Uncle Ron had gone back home in case Violet went there.

I decided to go up to my room. My mum and dad and Auntie Alice were all just sat in the living room, talking, planning what they intended to do the next day if Violet wasn't home.

I sat in my room, looking at Violet's stuff and her photos. I laid on my bed, praying for Violet.

I must have fallen asleep, because the next thing I remember was waking up to lots of noise. I looked at the time, and it was 5.30 am. I was still in my uniform.

I went downstairs to see what all the noise was about. Downstairs was full – there must have been everybody from the village in our house. Auntie was organising everybody into groups so that the four corners of our village could be searched. Larna's mum and Saskia's mum had set up Facebook and Instagram pages. It sounded like they had been working on it all night. They already had over 9,000 followers. The weather wasn't good – it was raining – but that hadn't put anybody off; everybody was suitably dressed in coats, hats and wellies.

Our house was like Stansted airport. I realised that I hadn't seen my mum and dad. I went into the living room and they were sitting in there. I could see that they hadn't been to sleep and that they felt how I felt. They were still in the same clothes as yesterday. Both my mum and dad looked terrible – worse than yesterday – and they were both in a daze as if they didn't know where they were, and at first they didn't notice that I'd walked into the room.

Then my dad looked at me and said, 'Are Reggie and Francis okay?'

I replied, 'I think they are still asleep. I'll go and check them now.' I ran upstairs and quietly went into Francis's room. They were still both fast asleep, so I quietly shut the door and went back downstairs to the living room.

'They're okay, Dad. Fast asleep.'

'Good girl, Bonnie,' said mum.

Auntie had finished her briefing and everybody was preparing to start searching. I felt very pleased that so many people had come to help but also very sad – so many mixed feelings, it's hard to explain. I decided to make my mum and dad a cup of tea with biscuits. Auntie was very busy. She's such an organised woman. Everybody she phoned yesterday was all rallying round; it was like a military operation. My Auntie is a very well respected lady in Peter's Green. She works a lot with the community and will do everything she can to help them, plus Auntie gives most of her free time to charity work. I'd never felt so lucky to have Auntie Alice and Uncle Ron as I did right then. Auntie Alice was on full steam and nothing was going to slow her down. Auntie has a sense of agency about her. She cannot say it, but I can see that she would like to tell everybody that Violet needs to be found TODAY.

Uncle Ron has always doted on Violet. Auntie told me she made Uncle Ron go to the hospital when my mum was having Violet. Uncle Ron arrived at the hospital just after Violet was born, and I think that's why Violet has a special place in his heart. I was dreading seeing Uncle Ron that morning. I was really worried for him. Uncle is much older than my mum and dad. If Violet wasn't found, it could seriously damage his health.

I went back upstairs to have a wash and change my clothes. I went to check on Reggie and Francis, and they were just waking up, so I got them both up, washed and dressed. They both looked very tired, and they didn't say much to me.

Then, after they were both dressed, Francis must have remembered, and said, 'Is Violet home?' and Reggie repeated her question.

I had to tell them that Violet wasn't back yet, and Reggie and Francis started to cry.

Francis said, 'Will we ever see Violet again?'

I replied, 'Everybody is doing everything they can to find Violet, so hopefully she will come home soon.'

Reggie and Francis went downstairs whilst I tried to tidy up their room. I hadn't eaten in ages and felt sick with weakness. After I'd washed and changed my clothes I went back downstairs and saw that the police had arrived to collect our phones. They told my mum and dad that it was now official: Violet was missing.

'We are checking all CCTV in the immediate area of the school,' one said.

The police wanted to talk to us, so we sat down in the kitchen.

'We will get straight to the point,' said the lady officer. 'Do you think that Violet's disappearance has anything to do with your group that you are involved with via social media?'

I sat for a minute and thought before I answered. I told the officers that if they would have asked me this question yesterday I would have said most definitely yes, but today I thought differently, and my answer was no. My friends from the group did speak to Violet on a couple of different occasions, and I knew they weren't kind to Violet and her friends, but I didn't think they had taken my sister from her family. I didn't think they were capable of that.

'Next question: Did Violet ever show any concerns about your friends?'

'Yes, Violet told me that she didn't like them very much. Violet said they was spiteful.'

'Next question: Did Violet have any confrontation with your friends?'

'Yes, just once that I know of, in the dinner room at school, because Violet and her friends are goths, and they are different. The girls were laughing at them, but it never seemed to bother Violet. She just thought they were ignorant.'

'Well, that's all the questions we have for now.'

The officers walked over to my mum and dad next. 'Do you mind if we ask you a couple of questions?'

My mum shook her head and said quietly, 'No.'

The lady officer said, 'Every question I ask you is for both of you. First question: Did you notice anything different about Violet's behaviour in the past few weeks?'

Both Mum and Dad replied, 'No.'

Next question: 'Has there been any upset in the family? And when I say family, I mean immediate and extended family.'

'No.'

'Have you had a chance to see if Violet as taken anything with her, i.e. extra clothes, money, etc?'

'No. We haven't been in her room. Violet shares her room with Bonnie.' Mum turned to me. 'Bonnie, have you noticed anything missing?'

I replied, 'At a glance, no, Mum.'

'Next question, are there any other family members that Violet knows and trusts that she might go and stay with, near or far?'

'No,' Mum replied. 'Both sets of our parents have passed on. Charlie's an only child, and I have one sister, Alice, and she lives just the other side of the green.'

'Okay, that's all for now. Please may we take a look in Violet's room?'

'Yes, of course. Bonnie will take you up to the room.'

I led the two police officers upstairs to see mine and Violet's room.

'Sorry about the mess,' I said.

'No worries, it's just so we can paint a picture of Violet.'

'Looking at these walls,' said the gentleman officer, 'someone has been doing plenty of painting pictures.'

'Yes,' I replied. 'That's Violet – she's the artist of the family.'

'Very good,' he replied. 'Does she sell any of these paintings?'

'Yes, I replied. 'Sometimes she does.'

'Talented girl,' said the lady officer.

'Yes, she is.'

'Just out of curiosity, how does she sell her paintings? Is it via the internet, on Facebook?

'No,' I replied. 'My Uncle Ron puts them in his gallery for her.'

'Uncle Ron? Is that Alice's husband?' said the lady officer.

'Yes.'

The officers nodded and started to peer around the room.

'Okay, well, I'll leave you to have a good look around. If you need anything just give me a shout I'm going back downstairs.'

'We will. Thank you,' the officers replied.

When I got back downstairs, Uncle Ron had just walked in, and he was making coffee for himself and Mum and Dad. Uncle Ron looked like he'd been up all night too. He asked me if Auntie Alice had come back from the search yet.

I shook my head. Uncle Ron looked so sad; none of us really knew which way to turn. I cannot explain how hard this situation is. You cannot take your eyes off the door because you're just expecting Violet to walk back in at any minute, and every minute seems like ten minutes. Even worse than that is feeling so hopeless. What can you do? Where can you go? Who can you talk to? What can you say? How do you feel? And there aren't any answers, just hopelessness.

I heard the police officers coming back down the stairs. They went into the living room to my mum and dad, and I heard them saying, 'That's all we can do for the time being. We're going back to the station now to see if there have been any developments.'

Before the police officers walked out, they looked round and noticed Uncle Ron, who was standing in the kitchen, drinking coffee. I introduced the police officers. 'This is my Uncle Ron that I was telling you about. Uncle Ron sells the paintings for Violet.'

Uncle Ron went straight over to them and shook their hands.

'Hello, Ron,' said the officers. 'Your niece Violet is very talented.'

'Yes, we are very proud of Violet,' he replied. 'Some of my customers think her paintings are amazing. Violet has even been commissioned by a couple of my customers to paint their children.'

'This situation is unbearable – we understand,' said the police officers. 'We want you to know that we are doing everything we can.'

'Thank you,' said Uncle Ron.

'Can we ask you, Ron, did you notice any change in Violet's behaviour?'

'No. Violet, along with the rest of the family, was at our place over the weekend.'

I was listening to the police officer and Uncle Ron talking, and then I remembered something and said it aloud: 'Violet has her own room at Auntie Alice and Uncle Ron's.'

'Yes,' said Uncle Ron, 'That's right.'

The police officers looked at Uncle Ron. 'Would you mind if we went over to your house and looked at Violet's room?'

'No,' said Uncle Ron.

'Let's go straight there now – oh wait, would you like to finish your coffee first?'

'No, definitely not. I never thought about Violet's room at our house. Would you like me to drive you over to our house?' said Uncle Ron.

The police officers replied, 'No need. We can just walk over there from here.'

And off they went.

*

8.30 am and Auntie Alice arrived back at our house. By then, everybody doing the search had gone to work, but Auntie made sure everybody had a photo of Violet to take with them.

Auntie couldn't sit still. 'Bonnie, would you make me a coffee, please? Grace, the school has just phoned me and they're going to do a special assembly at 10 am this morning. Mrs May has also asked me to tell you, and she also asked if you would like to come along too.'

'I don't think I'm up to that,' Mum replied.

'I didn't think so,' replied Auntie, 'but I thought it best to ask.'

'What will the assembly be about?' Mum asked.

'Well,' replied Auntie, 'judging by the quick conversation I had on the phone, they are going to let the whole school know that Violet is missing, and ask everybody to pray for Violet's safe return.'

Auntie then turned to me. 'Has Ron been over yet?'

'Yes,' I replied. 'He's taken the police officers over to your house to search Violet's room, in case there are any clues. They've already done our bedroom here.'

'Good idea,' said Auntie. 'I never thought to look in there when I went back last night. Mind you, probably best I didn't. Leave it to the experts.'

Auntie asked my mum and dad, 'Have you had anything to eat yet, you two?'

'No,' my mum replied.

'You should,' said Auntie. 'We all need to keep our strength up.'

With that, I decided to make some toast. Reggie and Francis had cereals earlier, but they asked me if they could have toast as well.

My mum asked Auntie, 'Did you find anything in your search, Alice?'

'No,' replied Auntie. 'I didn't expect to, if I'm honest, but it's a job that's now been done, and we can put that aside. Everybody was more than happy to help me.'

'Karen and Gina are having more luck with the Facebook page they set up,' Mum said. 'That seems to be gaining a lot of ground very quickly.'

'Has anybody told the police about that Facebook page?' Auntie asked.

My mum replied, 'No, I never thought about that.'

Auntie replied, 'When the police get back here, make sure you tell them before they go. I'm going now. Are you sure, Grace, that you don't want to come with me to the school?'

'Yes, I can't face all those children, but thank you very much anyway, and good luck.'

My dad hadn't moved from the living room yet that day. Reggie and Francis weren't going to school that day, neither was I, and my mum told my dad to go up to the bedroom and get some sleep. He agreed that this was a good idea and made his way upstairs. 'For a few hours,' he said as he walked up the stairs, 'and then I'm going back out in the car, because just sitting here is driving me crazy.'

*

After about an hour, Uncle Ron and the police officers came back to our house. I remembered to tell them what Auntie had said about the Facebook page which Karen and Gina had set up, which had already gained 9,000 followers. I continued, 'My auntie also told me to tell you that her search amounted to nothing, but it was done so now it could be put aside.'

The lady officer said, 'We are very grateful for all that your auntie is doing, but we will not put anything aside until Violet's found.'

I said to the police officers, 'Auntie means well. This is just her way of dealing with this situation.'

48

'We understand that,' said the police officer, 'and these types of situations are very hard to bear so it's best to just let your auntie get on with what she wants to do.'

Just before the officers left, they told me to tell my mum and dad that they were also going into the school that morning to speak to some of the pupils. They also told me to tell my mum and dad that they would not be back at the station until after 12 noon, and if there were any developments they would ring after then.

I thanked them, and they left.

I asked Uncle Ron if they'd found anything in Violet's room.

'No,' he replied. 'They didn't find anything. They mentioned Violet's paintings a couple of times, so I took them into my gallery and showed them the paintings on the wall that Violet had done. They were very impressed with Violet's paintings. They said they looked even nicer once they were in the frames. They had a good look around our place, and I let them search everywhere – they looked in every room upstairs, not just Violets, yours as well. "We have nothing to hide," I told them. "You can go anywhere you like." They thanked me.'

Uncle Ron look so tired. I made him a cup of tea and a piece of toast and he went into the living room and put on the TV. Within no time, he was fast asleep on the settee.

Reggie and Francis had gone into the garden to play. Just then, Saskia and Larna came round to see me, so we all sat in the garden, watching the two little ones play whilst we were talking. I was glad of their company, but at the same time I really wanted them to leave me alone – but if I'm honest, the loneliness is unbearable. I can't explain how I felt in this situation. You can't pinpoint anything that you want, or you can see, or you know, it's just a numb feeling of nothing. The only thing that you are sure of is that you want your sister to walk back in the house with a big smile on her face and say, 'Hello, everybody. I'm home.'

*

Once my dad and Uncle Ron woke up, they both decided to go out in the car again and have a look round.

Gina and Karen came to see my mum. Gina had taken the day off work to help with the search and the Facebook page, which was going well. Karen and Gina decided they would cook something to eat.

Mum smiled weakly. 'Nice idea, but I'm struggling to eat a piece of toast.'

'We will make cottage pie and lasagna, and you can eat them when you're ready.'

Mum told them that was a good idea.

We were very lucky to have all this support. It somehow made the time go quicker, but then I didn't want the time to go quicker; I wanted the time to stand still so Violet could catch up. *Yes, that's what I wanted: time to stand still*, I thought to myself. *Run fast, Violet, and you will catch up. We're all here, waiting for you.* Yes, that's something I was sure about. I definitely wanted time to stand still.

My mum was very lucky to have such good friends. Karen was making cottage pie, and Gina was making lasagna. Saskia and Larna were keeping Reggie and Francis occupied, and my mum was trying to tidy up the living room, but I could see she was really struggling.

I went into deep thought about where my sister was. I started to imagine that she could be walking around the town or in the shops, looking at new clothes, maybe even trying them on, or sat in the restaurant on her own, having a cup of tea and just sitting there thinking about coming home.

Where are you, Violet? Have you gone to the cinema and not told anybody? Have you gone to the leisure centre to meet your friends in secret? Are you walking in the park or playing on the swings? Have you met up with someone, maybe old friends, and gone to a museum? Have you taken the train and gone to another town? Maybe you're walking to another town? Have you decided to go on a long train journey, maybe around the east coast? I don't know really where you are, Violet, but I have my fingers crossed and I'm praying with all my heart that you are just going to walk back in through that door at any minute now. I'm watching. I'm watching that door. Please, Violet, please just come back home. We can't bear it without you. It's breaking our hearts.

*

Auntie Alice arrived back at our house. I hoped that she had something else to do. If Auntie sat down, I was afraid she may not get back up.

'Grace, I need to talk to you privately,' she said to my mum.

Hearing Auntie say that made me feel worse.

My mum and Auntie went upstairs. Gina and Karen were still cooking, and Larna and Saskia were still in the garden, keeping an eye on Reggie and Francis. My dad and Uncle Ron were still out in the car. Where did that leave me? Nowhere.

I quickly ran upstairs. I was feeling angry. I walked straight into my mum's bedroom. Auntie and my mum went quiet and looked at me, and just like that I said, 'I want to know what you're talking about. Violet's my sister, and I want to know everything that's going on.'

My mum looked at me, and she could see I was upset. 'You're right, Bonnie. We shouldn't have left you downstairs. Sorry, I wasn't thinking.'

Auntie started talking again. 'When I got to the school, Rose called me straight into her office. She had been there for hours, going through the CCTV footage. She'd gone back to the

51

beginning of last week. Bonnie, your friends had been chatting to Violet every day last week just before dinner.'

'Were they bullying her?' I asked.

Auntie replied, 'From what I can see, it doesn't look that way. They look like they're just talking.'

Mum looked at me. 'Did Violet say anything to you about chatting to your friends?'

'No, nothing. The only thing Violet mentioned to me was when we were in the kitchen the other day, when she said they were spiteful.'

'That's right. I remember.'

Then Auntie went on. 'Yesterday, again they were chatting to Violet before dinner, and from the CCTV footage you can see that Violet is stressed, and they handed her a little package, and then you see them walk away. Violet never went into the dinner room. Violet walked straight out of school at 12.05, and that was the last time Violet was seen by the CCTV. Violet never returned to school yesterday.'

'How big was the package?' Mum asked.

'From what we could see, about 4 cm square.'

My mum asked, 'Was it cigarettes?'

'No, definitely not cigarettes. The package was wrapped in brown paper.'

I asked Auntie, 'Do you know if they are in school today?'

'Yes, all four of them.'

'Do the police know this information?' asked Mum.

'Yes. The police were waiting for their parents to arrive so they could show them the footage before the school day ends. The police want to show the girls the footage with their parents present so there are no excuses. If they can get that done before the end of the school day, this should shed some light on Violet's whereabouts. All the parents have promised to be there before the end of school today, and the police are staying with the girls until their parents arrive.'

My mum breathed out a sigh of relief. 'Well, that sounds hopeful.'

'Yes, said Auntie, 'but let's keep it to ourselves for now.' Auntie yawned. 'I'm going to try and get some sleep for an hour or two.'

We went back downstairs, and Gina and Karen asked us whether everything was okay. My mum replied, 'Yes, nothing significant. Alice just wanted to explain what Mrs May told her in confidence. The school is doing all they can to help.'

'That's fantastic,' said Karen. 'Mrs May is a very nice lady.'

'Yes, she is. Alice went to school with Rose,' my mum told them, 'so they are old friends.'

'Something smells nice,' I said. 'It's the first time I've felt hungry in the past twenty-four hours.'

'Do you want any cottage pie?' Karen asked me, 'because it's ready.'

'Yes please.'

Gina asked my mum, 'Is Alice having a sleep?'

'Yes,' Mum replied. 'I don't know how she keeps up.'

Karen asked, 'What has Alice done with the shop?'

'Two of her friends from dance club heard about Violet and offered to look after the shop. They've done it once before so they know what they're doing. Lucky, really.'

Karen said, 'Everybody worships Alice in Peter's Green. She's like the "Queen of our Green".'

My mum replied, 'She only keeps that shop open for the older generation. Alice hardly makes any money from the shop.'

Gina said, 'She has the biggest heart I've ever seen.'

Reggie and Francis came back in, followed by Saskia and Larna. We all sat down and had cottage pie and baked beans. Since Auntie told me what had happened at school, I felt a bit better, and my mum had a glimmer of hope on her face.

Just then, some of Violet's friends from the green came over to see if there was any news. I told them how the police were here first thing and how they had checked everything they needed to, how my dad and uncle were out, looking round. Last of all, I told them how we had over 9,000 followers on Facebook.

'Yes, we've seen that. It's amazing how the word gets around so quickly.'

'It seems everybody is looking everywhere, except me. I feel so useless,' I said.

'You shouldn't say that.'

'I know, but I can't help it.'

I made them all a cup of tea, and we sat for a while, chatting, and then one of them said, 'Look, you know where we are if you need anything.'

I nodded. 'Thanks again for your support. It means a lot to us.'

*

My dad and Uncle Ron returned: no Violet and nothing to report. They both looked terrible.

Auntie Alice awoke from her sleep and came back downstairs. Mum, Dad, Auntie and Uncle, Reggie and Francis were all now sitting in the living room together, and every one of us, including me, all looked like death warmed up. We had been completely turned on our heads. Auntie was out of the shop, my dad's deliveries had all been postponed, my mum's dressmaking had come to a complete stop, Uncle Ron had just closed up shop until further notice, Reggie and Francis were not at school, and Violet was still not home, and it was 3.30 pm the day after Violet went missing. Gina, Karen, Saskia and Larna had all left. I felt like we were sat in an empty shell with no way out.

Then we heard a car pull up outside. It was the police. We all filled with dread. My mum, started to cry, my dad stood straight up, Uncle Ron put his head in his hands, and Auntie

Alice braced herself to face the music. She was the only one that looked somewhere near capable of listening to what the police were going to say.

I got Reggie and Francis and quickly took them upstairs and put the TV on.

Francis asked me, 'Are the police bringing Violet home?'

I replied, 'Let's wait and see.'

I went back downstairs and I had that suffocating feeling again. I couldn't breathe.

Auntie Alice was holding herself up by the worktop. I could see her knuckles had gone white. She was holding on for dear life. Uncle Ron still had his head in his hands, and my dad was still standing but couldn't stop shaking. My mum was still slightly crying.

Finally the police officers got to our door. It seemed like it had taken them forever to walk up our drive, and then the knock on the door came.

Auntie walked towards the door. Everything was silent, as if we were all holding our breath – well, the reality was that we were. The door opened, and two police officers walked in. The first thing I noticed was that they weren't the same two officers that were here that morning.

No one said anything. Then one of the officers spoke. 'It's GOOD NEWS.'

I wanted to kiss the officers. I felt like someone had taken the roof off our house and let all the bad vibes out. And then came the emotion called happiness – yes, happiness. We all thought we were never going to experience that ever again. When I looked round, everybody – even the lady officer – was crying with relief. Uncle Ron and my mum were hugging each other. I ran upstairs to tell Reggie and Francis that Violet had been found. Reggie and Francis ran straight downstairs and gave Dad a big hug, then everybody else.

Auntie, who was the only one still standing in the same position, quickly asked, 'How is Violet?'

Nobody had considered her well-being in that moment; we were just glad she was alive.

The officer replied, 'Very well, and unharmed. We were going to phone you and let you know that Violet was okay, but Violet wouldn't allow us to do that. Violet wanted us to tell you in person, so we could assure you that she is okay.'

My dad asked, 'Can Violet come home?'

'Yes, but we need to question Violet, so one of you will need to come down to the station.'

My mum looked unsure. 'Is Violet in trouble?'

'No. However, Violet has been involved in the delivery of drugs.'

Our happiness started to fade, and one by one a look of shock appeared on our faces, and everyone was now staring at me.

The officer said, 'Look, Violet is unharmed, but she's very tired and we would like to get this cleared up so Violet can come home. At this point, there is nothing to worry about, so please can we make our way to the station? If one of you can come with us, we can explain to you on the way.'

'Yes, yes,' said my mum nervously, grabbing her bag.

Mum and Dad got into the police car, and Uncle Ron followed behind with his car, and within seconds they were gone. As soon as they were gone, Auntie started to phone round to tell everybody Violet had been found safe and well, thanking them for their support. Auntie phoned the shop to let her friends know that Violet had been found safe and well, and to ask her friends if they could stay on for the rest of the week and look after the shop. Auntie Alice had a look of relief on her face once she'd told everyone. 'Okay, Bonnie, let's get nicely tidied up now, so when Violet comes home everything is as nice as it can be.'

We quickly got everything ready for Violet to come home. We couldn't wait to see Violet, and I wanted to tell her I was sorry for bringing such spiteful people into our lives.

*

After a few hours we heard Uncle Ron's car. Reggie and Francis were screaming, 'Violet's back! Violet's back!'

'Okay, you two, calm down,' said Auntie.

And just like that, Violet walked through the door.

Reggie and Francis ran straight to Violet and wrapped their arms around her as tightly as they could. 'Violet! We've missed you!' they shrieked.

I looked at Violet and my eyes started to fill. We both walked towards each other. We wrapped our arms around each other as if we had not seen each other for years, I felt like I couldn't let go.

'I'm so sorry, Violet.'

'It's not your fault, Bonnie. They're bad people, and now they're in a lot of trouble.'

I could see Violet was very tired.

'If you don't mind, I'm going to have a shower and get to bed,' she said.

As Violet walked up the stairs, I looked around at the rest of the family. Everybody looked ten years younger than they had done a few hours earlier.

One thing I was sure of was that we would all sleep better that night.

'I do have one question though,' I said.

Everybody looked round at me. 'What's that, Bonnie?'

'How did we get Violet back?'

My mum replied, 'Well, it's a very long story, but what I can confirm is that Sacha's mum was instrumental in Violet's safe return.'

Lightning Source UK Ltd.
Milton Keynes UK
UKHW030716141020
371555UK00001B/46